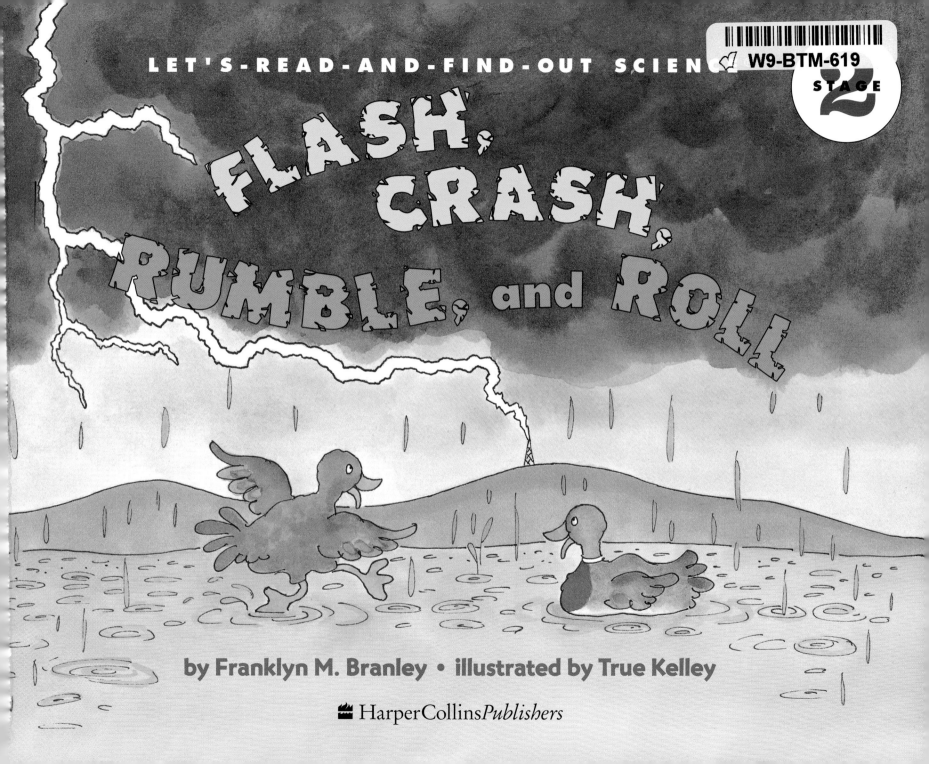

A special thanks to Chris Strong
at the National Weather Service
for his expert advice

The illustrations in this book were done in watercolor and pen and ink on Fabriano watercolor paper.

The *Let's-Read-and-Find-Out Science* book series was originated by Dr. Franklyn M. Branley, Astronomer Emeritus and former Chairman of the American Museum–Hayden Planetarium, and was formerly co-edited by him and Dr. Roma Gans, Professor Emeritus of Childhood Education, Teachers College, Columbia University. Text and illustrations for each of the books in the series are checked for accuracy by an expert in the relevant field. For more information about Let's-Read-and-Find-Out Science books, write to HarperCollins Children's Books, 10 East 53rd Street, New York, NY 10022, or visit our web site at http://www.harperchildrens.com.

HarperCollins®, 📖®, and Let's Read-and-Find-Out Science® are trademarks of HarperCollins Publishers Inc.

FLASH, CRASH, RUMBLE, AND ROLL

Library of Congress Cataloging-in-Publication Data
Branley, Franklyn Mansfield, 1915–
    Flash, crash, rumble, and roll / by Franklyn M. Branley ; illustrated by True Kelley. — Rev. ed., newly illustrated.
        p.   cm. — (Let's-read-and-find-out science. Stage 2)
    Summary: Explains how and why a thunderstorm occurs and gives safety steps to follow when lightning is flashing.
    ISBN 0-06-027858-7. — ISBN 0-06-027859-5 (lib. bdg.)
    ISBN 0-06-445179-8 (pbk.)
    1. Thunderstorms—Juvenile literature. [1. Thunderstorms. 2. Lightning—Safety measures. 3. Safety.] I. Kelley,
True, ill. II. Title. III. Series.
QC968.B73   1999   97-43599
551.55'4—dc21   CIP
                                                                                                                              AC

1 2 3 4 5 6 7 8 9 10
❖
Newly Illustrated Edition

The day is quiet. The air is still and hot. Leaves do not move. Flowers droop. Even the birds are still and quiet. There are big white clouds in the sky.

Picnic!

They grow bigger and taller. And they get darker and darker.

"Look at those black thunderclouds," people say. "We're going to have a thunderstorm."

Warm air near the earth is rising
into the clouds. The air goes up fast.

Inside the clouds it keeps moving
upward. It may go all the way to the
top and spill over.

The clouds keep growing. After a
while the clouds may be ten miles high.

ice
crystals

water
drops

water
vapor

The rising air carries water. But it's not liquid. It is a gas called water vapor. When water vapor cools, it becomes liquid water. That's what happens in the clouds to make them grow. Water vapor cools and changes into small drops of water, and also into small crystals of ice.

COLDER
AIR

very cold

very cold

warming

warming

Air inside the cloud carries the water and ice up and up.

The air gets colder.

When it gets very cold, the air falls.

So the air inside some parts of a cloud is moving up very fast, and in other parts it is moving down.

Planes stay out of these dark thunderclouds. The rushing air could turn a plane upside down. It could even rip off the wings.

Also, there's electricity in the clouds. Each water droplet and ice crystal carries a tiny bit of electricity.

There are billions and billions of droplets and crystals. So the amount of electricity gets greater and greater.

When the amount is very great, the electricity jumps from the top of the cloud to the very bottom. It makes a giant spark—a flash of lightning.

Meanwhile the rain starts. First only a drop or two.
Then the wind blows, and the rain falls faster and harder.
Water races down the street. There's more lightning. It
may go from one cloud to another.

Or it may reach a high building or a tree. The streak of lightning may be a mile long or even longer.

Thunder comes after the lightning. The lightning is very hot. It heats the air. The hot air expands very fast. It makes sound waves all along the streak of lightning.

The sound waves reach you at different times. When the first one reaches your ears, there may be a loud crash. As more and more sound waves reach you, the thunder rumbles and rolls.

CRASH!

RUMBLE RUMBLE

ROLL ROLL

You make sound waves when you break a balloon.

Blow one up and pop it. The air in the balloon expanded rapidly through the break in the skin. You made a tiny bit of thunder.

There's only a little air in the balloon, so there's not much noise. Lightning moves lots more air—billions of times more—so there is lots of sound.

Sound waves travel slowly, much more slowly than the light from lightning.

Light travels so fast, it can go to the moon in less than two seconds. It would take two weeks for sound to go that far.

Because light goes so fast, you see lightning the moment it flashes. But it may take several seconds for the thunder to reach you. It takes 5 seconds for the sound to travel 1 mile.

The next time you see lightning, try this: Count the seconds until you hear the thunder.

If 5 seconds go by, the storm is 1 mile away. If 10 seconds pass, the storm is 2 miles away. If only a second passes, the storm is very close.

If you see a flash and you don't hear thunder at all, the storm may be 15 miles or more away.

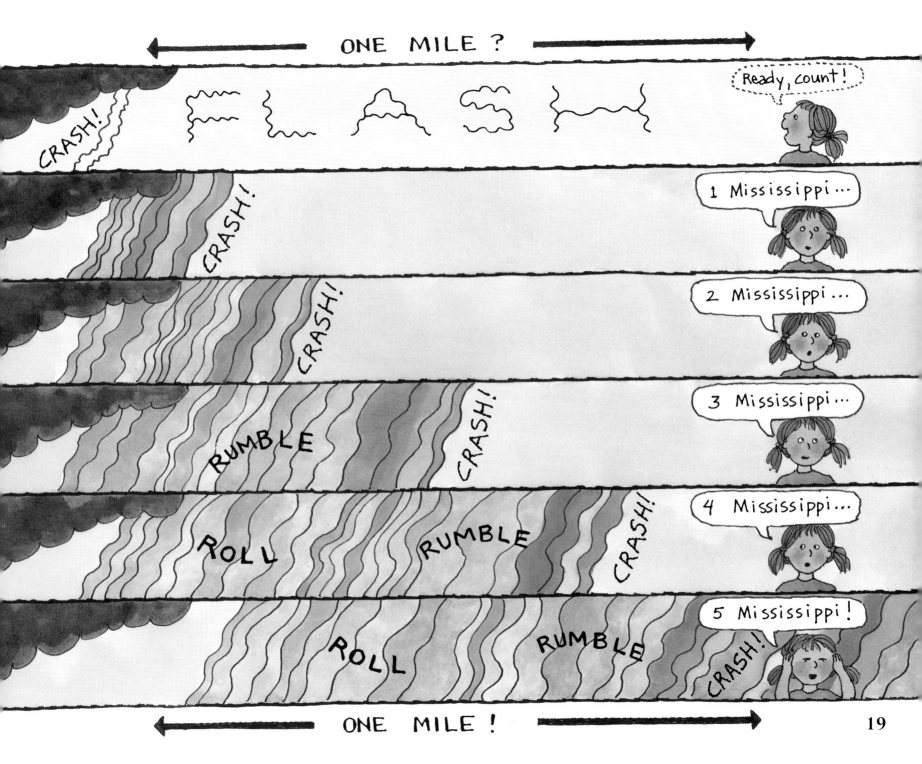

The thunder will be very loud. It may be scary, but thunder won't hurt you.

Lightning is different.

Lightning may start fires in houses or barns. It may start forest fires. Lightning may knock over trees and telephone poles. It may kill cows and horses in a field. It may injure people or kill them.

You won't be hurt by lightning if you know what to do.

If you are swimming, get out of the water.

If you are outside, go inside.

If you are inside when a storm is close, stay away from the telephone and the TV. Their wires could carry lightning into the house.

Stay away from the stove and other big metal things.

Stay away from sinks, the bathtub, and the shower. Their pipes could also carry lightning into the house.

If you are inside when a storm is close, stay away from the telephone and the TV. Their wires could carry lightning into the house.

Stay away from the stove and other big metal things.

Stay away from sinks, the bathtub, and the shower. Their pipes could also carry lightning into the house.

If you are caught outdoors, keep away from a metal fence, or metal pipes. They could carry electricity.

Don't stand under a tree that is alone in a field. Lightning usually strikes the highest thing. It might strike the tree.

So if you're in a big field, don't be the highest thing around. Crouch down, with your knees on the ground, and bend your head forward.

If you are in a car, stay there. A car is safe, because if lightning hits it, the electricity goes through the car and not through you.

Watch the storm from a safe place. Before it begins, watch the clouds. You'll see them get bigger and bigger, taller and taller, darker and darker.

You'll see flashes of lightning. If the storm is far away, you'll hear thunder rumble and roll. If it's close by, the thunder will crackle and crash.

People used to think that lightning was the fiery fingers of an angry god. They thought the god made thunder when he scolded and roared.

They feared storms as they feared their gods.

But there's no reason for us to fear storms. We know what makes thunder and lightning. And we know how to keep safe.

chirp!

- **Make a rain gauge**

  You will need a clear plastic bottle, scissors, a ruler, a permanent marker, and paper.

  1. Ask an adult to help you cut the plastic bottle in half.

  2. Using the ruler and marker, make several marks at quarter-inch intervals going up the bottle.

  3. Next time there is a storm, place your rain gauge in the open (not near a building or under a tree). To keep it from blowing away, you might attach it to a stake. After the storm is over, record how much water is in your rain gauge. Then empty the container.

  4. Repeat step three after each storm for a month. Compare your findings with the average monthly rainfall for your area or the recorded rainfall for a particular storm.

- **Make a cloud**

  You will need a few ice cubes, a dash of salt, a saucer, a glass jar, and some hot water.

  1. Place the ice cubes and salt in the saucer. (The salt helps the ice melt quickly, so the saucer becomes very cold.)

  2. Rinse the jar in hot water. Then fill it halfway with hot water.

  3. Place the saucer over the mouth of the jar.

  You will see a misty cloud quickly form between the water and the saucer as the warm water evaporates, then meets the cool air near the ice cubes and condenses.

  After a minute or so, lift up the saucer and look at the bottom. You'll notice it is covered with drops of water. If they fell, they would be just like raindrops.

- **Visit these weather sites on the Internet:**

  http://autobrand.wunderground.com for global forecasts, average temperatures, and radar maps.

  http://www.storm-track.com for storm information, images, and tracking.

  http://www.weather.com/education/ for the hows, whys, and wonders of weather.